Granny and the Monster

By Rob and Celia Carlile

First edition published in 2016
ISBN - 13: 978-1530139354
ISBN - 10: 153013935X

We would like to acknowledge
Aaron O'Driscoll for his technical support.

This is a story about a boy named Billy and his granny.

Billy's granny is different to a lot of other grannies.

She doesn't drink tea, she drinks smoothies.

She doesn't watch soap operas, she watches monster movies.

But Billy's granny does one thing that lots of grannies do. Billy's granny loves to knit. She knits all day, every day. She would knit for ever and ever if she could.

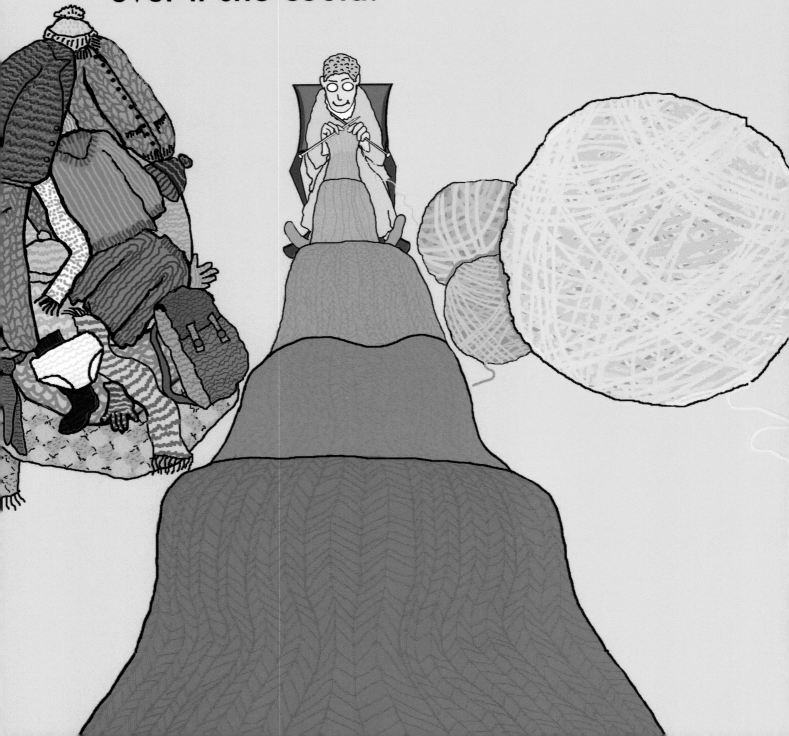

Granny knitted all of Billy's clothes.

The only problem is...

Billy doesn't like wearing knitted clothes all the time.

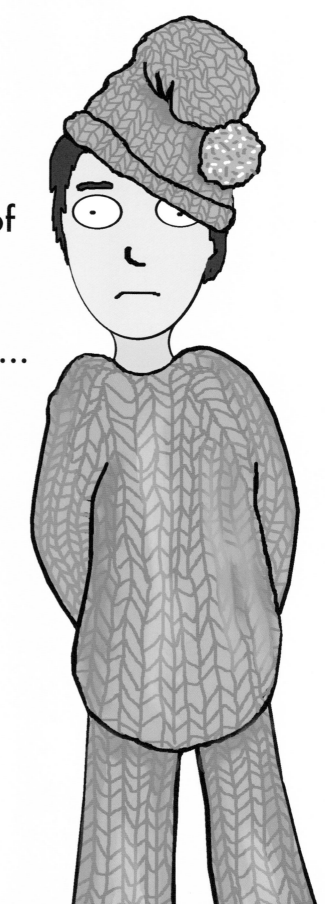

One day Billy was playing with a football.

He kicked the ball so high and so far that it went over a wall.

Billy climbed carefully over the wall.
He saw the ball caught in a bush.

When he lifted the ball, he saw
something very strange underneath.

It was some kind of monster.

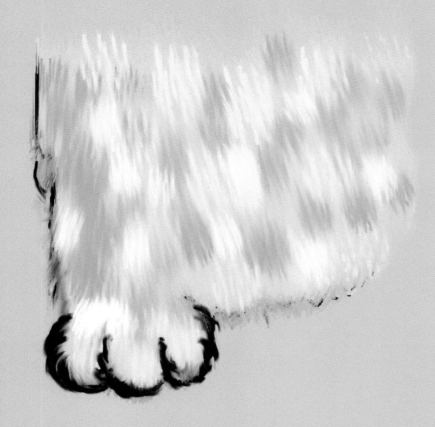

It had soft fur,
like a blanket.

It had round eyes,
like marbles.

Billy felt very sorry that his ball had hit the monster.

Billy picked up the little monster and carried him home.

The monster looked sick.

Billy brought it some fruit.

Billy brought it some vegetables.

Billy brought it some chicken.
The little monster wouldn't eat anything.

Billy made the monster a bed out
of a blanket that Granny had knit.

The next morning when Billy woke up the monster was standing on Billy's bed. He didn't look sick anymore. He looked healthy and happy. He wasn't grey anymore, now he was purple. The purple blanket that Billy had given him had disappeared.

Just then Granny called Billy. She had
knitted him a new scarf. He stepped out of
the room and shut the door behind him.
He didn't want Granny to see the monster.

When Billy went back into his
bedroom he got a fright. The monster
was eating one of Billy's jumpers.

Billy had to go to school, but he couldn't leave the monster in his house. Billy put the monster into his schoolbag and closed it. When Billy got to school he opened his bag to see if the monster was okay.

There was a hole in the bag.
The monster was missing.

Billy was worried all day in school. What if the monster was in the house?
It had been eating everything. What if it had eaten Granny?

When school was over
Billy ran home as fast
as he could.

When he got home he pushed open the door and saw...

Granny and the monster!

Granny said the monster was the best thing ever. She said she loved having her own real-life monster.
She wanted to call him Stitch. She said that Stitch loved her knitting more than anyone.

Granny knitted all kinds of things for Stitch to eat. At dinner time she'd knit a dinner for Stitch too.

Granny was happy, and with loads of knitting to eat, the monster was happy too.

Since Granny was so busy knitting for Stitch, she didn't have time to knit all of Billy's clothes.

Billy got to wear all the different kinds of clothes that he wanted. Billy was very happy.

My Granny Knits

Orison Carlile

Listen to the song at celiacarlile.com

Printed in Great Britain
by Amazon